# Yes.
# Every Single Day.

## Stephanie Logue

To summer and country music
late at night on your radio.

# The Beginning

It's late in the afternoon. Maybe a Tuesday? We still have a few minutes until the screen door squeaks to announce one of my parents is home from work, but time is on our side for now.

Sunlight paints the walls orange-yellow through my mom's white curtains from the JCPenney catalog. A web of laced shadow drapes over the carpet above our heads. I itch to walk my fingers in the tatting's outline, searching for a path from the maze. But it's a moving target; the lace rises and settles back; the windows are open, and breathing.

We lay on the floor, side-by-side. I hope my hair fans behind me like a mermaid. You place your open palm into mine. Your skin is softer than I imagined. Boys are supposed to have rough skin, especially boys like you, with your hard shell and perma-frown behind the wheel of the eighties coupe that saw its better days before we got our drivers licenses. But your palm is soft, even if I'm too nervous to grasp on, instead holding still and hoping to every entity I can pinpoint in my swirling thoughts that you aren't about to see your folly, get up, and run away. Or that I don't panic and do the same. Dreams coming true — I don't know what those look like. I don't think you do either.

But you stay. So I do too.

"Can I kiss you?" Your voice dips, and rises, like a roller coaster. It's the second time you've ever sounded nervous, at least to me. The first was yesterday, when you lingered at the end of my checkout line, next to a stand of red-, white-, and blue-wrapped Hershey Kisses. The little tinfoils gleamed under the artificial lights, and the chocolate probably melted as you manhandled the bag, marble-mouthing your way around asking me to the fireworks in a few days.

I say yes. To the fireworks, and to the kiss.

We're seventeen.

We've known each other for six years.

It's yes, every single day.

A fly buzzes, ramming into the window screen, thinking it found escape. My cocker spaniel twitches a floppy ear and shifts, his tailbone bumping the coffee table right where he likes it. I wonder if you can see my chest vibrating from my heart trying to escape.

We look at each other, as if we're entering upon an agreement. A student loan, a mortgage, a marriage certificate, of sorts. Sign here on the dotted line. We're just dumb kids: a teenage dirtbag and the yearbook editor. Headstrong mechanic and bookish nerd. Brown, messy hair with a curl at the end, and a blonde with the Valley Girl lilt to match. The tropes that work in books, but never in real life. Kisses should be fun and spontaneous and experimental, but this feels bigger. It'll be more. The beginning of everything that's gonna matter. Everything that's gonna stick to our ribs and define what's next.

Some might call this moment life-altering.

But we're still seventeen, cuddled close on the carpet, awkward, nervous weirdos, filled with hormones and questions we don't have words for yet.

Your wrist is trapped under my hip. The carpet is itchy on my cheek and I remember Mom asked me to vacuum the dog fur before I let anyone in the house.

That's what I'm thinking about when our lips touch. I don't kiss you back; it's too overwhelming, your bottom lip moving against mine, delicate in the right way, like this was all you've ever wanted to do. Your chest touches mine, your free hand finds its way to my cheek, and I always wondered if that'd be weird, getting kissed and face-cradled. But it's not. It's nice. It's just you. And it's just me. Our two parallel stories converging, finally.

I can't remember if it was a Tuesday. Or what happened after the kiss. Did I scamper behind you to your car, our fingers knotted together already the second we heard my back door open? How many journal pages did I fill, trying to capture the feeling of the bees buzzing in my lungs as they fluttered between my ribs, weaving, spiking, flapping against muscle? How many words were dedicated to how I'd never sit still again because you finally kissed me, and how that energy did something to the way blood flowed through my veins?

All I remember is that when the kiss ends, you linger. Your fingertips inch into my hair, my eyelashes bookend your nose, and you funnel air in through your lips like you'd been holding your breath this whole time. The sound of your breathing, labored, no … nervous, splits me in two, and I know the part of me that cracks away attaches to you. Nothing could ever happen to you. I would never be the same. I will never be the same. If this is what I think it is…

Yeah. It is.

Fuck.

:::

You say you have a surprise for me.

It's late. Like, 11 o'clock late. Dad's gonna be pissed when he finds out his best girl was in the lilac bushes by the front door, webbing her fingers through yours so even the pale skin between each knuckle touched. This summer, I don't have enough skin; every part of me that touches you sparks like lightning, the crack of thunder reverberating through me right after.

Your car idles down the block. (Because: my dad.) Aerosmith blasts through the doors — Love in an Elevator — and we run to the car and speed off. Your car smells like metal and grease and the soft Tootsie Rolls you keep next to the gear shift for me. I crank down my window, my fingers gliding through the wind. When we run out of streetlights, you turn onto the county highway.

"There's a sleeping bag in the trunk." You hold my hand and kiss it, right under my middle knuckle. If I want a tattoo — which I don't, until this very second — that's what I'd get. An outline of your lips on my hand, forever and ever.

"It's not December," I say. That's our agreement. I will lose my virginity on our six-month anniversary. It feels adult to plan it, and responsible to be prepared. I may or may not have a countdown in my school planner. When I started counting backwards from One Day, I confidently wrote the numbers in ink and didn't think twice about it.

Now, I press my palm into your cheek as some sort of consolation prize. Here, you may have the inside of my hand, but you may not stick your fingers all the way inside my panties. Some semblance of bodily autonomy is key — I'd learned that on MTV during a Very Special Episode of TRL when Carson Daly propped himself on a stool in a dark studio, rather than being surrounded by a throng of screaming high schoolers. Autonomy is a new word in my vocabulary. I only read it, so I don't know where the pronunciation emphasis goes. You wouldn't either, so at least I won't look stupid.

In the dashboard glow, you lean into my hand and my heart threatens to jump ship and land in my lap. Your stubble is black and spiky, like a cactus. I love touching it when we kiss.

The beard prickle makes you real. (I'm still afraid that you're not.)

"A sleeping bag does not mean sex, my dear." You kiss the inside of my palm.

I can't decide which part of your superlative I love more: the name, or the claim that I'm yours. You call me honey. Sweetheart. Baby Girl. Woman. I'm not partial. If 'my' comes before any of them, I'm spellbound. We're two old souls full of sweet nothings, crashing through curfew in the middle of the night.

It's perfect. You're perfect.

"I mean." You laugh, and it catches the breeze. "If you really want to, I'm not gonna argue." Your peaceful smile radiates through the mostly-dark car. It's heartrending. It stops time. (How I wish it did.)

I laugh and shake my head. There's more research to be done. More preparation on my part. I've read it's a mind game as much as physical one for some girls, and I definitely categorize myself as Some Girls.

But damn. I want it to be you.

You slow the car and turn off the highway. The smell of lake water permeates the air. It's mossy. Sweet, like mildew, but no one cares because all it's doing is squelching algae to rocks as the lake sways from boats crisscrossing the water on Saturday afternoons.

The tires crunch over gravel, then weeds, and we stop. We get out of the car, and I hear the keys crash into a pile as you toss them on the seat. The night is black; I can barely see you popping the trunk. "Where are we?"

"That fishing spot I found that night I was late."

My eyes begin to adjust; I see your outline, gray and feet from me. Your arms puff around your stomach. You're holding the sleeping bag.

"Oh," I say. I remember that suffocating hour a few days ago when I didn't know where you were. I perched on the window ledge inside Mom's lace curtains like a cat stalking the resident squirrel, waiting for you to round the corner, for your headlights to sweep over our lilac bushes, for you to rescue me from the crushing reality of being alone in my head. Being alone sucks. It provides me the opportunity to invent stories, sometimes rooted in truth, sometimes not, that all snowball into you leaving and offering no explanation as to why.

You hold your hand out to me. That motion of reaching for me, your square nails and dirty knuckles permanently dusted with grit from stocking groceries on Wednesday and Thursday after school and tinkering on your car every other night, thrills me to my bone marrow. No one has ever made me a priority like you.

Into the brush we go. I grip your hand, then the inside of your elbow, moving gingerly to make sure my next step lands on solid ground. You know where we're going. Or at least you act like it.

"Here," you announce, as if we own the land we stand on. Like we're on the moon, and you have a flag to plant. You drop the sleeping bag, unroll it, and look at me. "You first."

I kick off my flip flops and take the creased side. You pull off your sneakers and slide in, offering your arm as a pillow. Flipping the top half of the sleeping bag over us, I press against you, my head on your shoulder, leg between your knees. Your jeans are wet from dragging in the dew. My fingertips drum into your ribs, until you thread our fingers together, stilling me.

This is the first time I count the places our bodies overlap.

I poke my nose skyward. "Why are we here?"

"You wanted to see a shooting star." Your voice is scratchy, like you've forgotten how to use it.

A few days ago, we'd brainstormed cheap date ideas, spooning on the couch in the basement under a blanket pulled up to our chins. Upstairs, your mother paced the kitchen floor, the pads of her feet sticking to the linoleum as she talked to your father on the cordless. Her voice was low, and somehow carried both quiet rage and despondency. She kept saying she was sorry, so sorry, over and over. Your dad emptied his hunting equipment and tools from the garage, took down his white head deer trophy in the basement, and moved out the next day.

I don't want to think about it.

You don't either.

So. We look up.

And boy, it's worth it. In the middle of town in the dead of night, I can only see one of the dippers. I never know which one it is. Even the full moon is dull hovering over the streetlights, as if it's shifting through its phases out of habit and not the greatest feat of light and shadow known to mankind.

The stars at the lake, though: I see everything. Layers of constellations, stacked like rice paper, thin enough to see through. Stars are bright white and cool, like glitter in the snow after a blizzard. Beyond, hazy dots blend into one, like sea waves. The universe is threads of blankets, weaving around us without ever acknowledging our tiny existence from billions of light years away.

It's too much. My average little brain can't process a bit of it, and I have questions. Questions on questions on questions. What did this piece of muddy sand we're sprawled on look like when this light saw its first glimmer? Was Earth even here? Did the starlight shoot from its stars, expecting to see dinosaurs? The Ice Age?

How is everyone in all the lake homes around us not wandering outside every night to see this? How are they not stuck in their yards, looking up in total awe, losing track of time and to-do lists as they contemplate how tiny, how insignificant our lives are? How bonkers is it that this is above us, every single day, and no one even cares?

But we care. We're here to see it. It's just me and you, right here, taking in this show. My heart sinks with the scariest thing I've ever thought: what happens to all the light that defies space and time, just to get to boring old here, and no one even sees it?

This light spent a literal eternity to get here, just to be…wasted. To have no one applaud its beauty or use it to catch someone else's smile. It just stops existing, crashing into Earth's crust, and is soaked down into the planet's belly.

And I thought Romeo and Juliet was the height of tragedy.

Your fingers brush my hip, just under my shirt. I shift to see you; you're the only reason to look away from the masterpiece in the sky.

"I need…" You cough into your fist, and the stars highlight how pale your face has gone. "I need to tell you. You make me feel more than any of the other girls I've dated. I think I'm in love with you." You pause, and dip your face to me. "I know I'm in love with you."

I've been in love with you since we were fourteen. Look at you. You're vulnerable and funny and your heart is about three times too big for your body. You love your mom and admire your dad, and you hold my hand like I'm something special. Of course I love you.

We kiss until we're dizzy even though we're flat on the ground. When you pull back, my lips are swollen and your hairline is damp. "We came here to watch the stars, my dear."

I settle against the inside of your elbow, and smile so you know I'm kidding. "No more kissing," I say. I see how it is."

You tilt my chin up, and the bees are back, tumbling through my insides. "I am always going to want to kiss you. But I found the best star-watching beach in the county."

We look up and let the light come to us.

:::

Go, go, go.

Your knee bounces under popcorn bags at the movies. Palms grind into your steering wheel at red lights. You're agitated all summer. Your dad moves to the Black Hills in July. Your mom stays here, to keep you and your brother in the same schools. I'm so grateful. And selfish. If I think about it too long, my skin feels too small.

I spend the summer losing entire pens to the pages in my journals and filling the space next to you as we drive. Wind tangles my hair so badly that I spray leave-in conditioner and yank a fine-tooth comb through the ends at night before bed. Once, I consider taking the kitchen shears to a knot, but feel that rumble in my gut that come before regret, and walk away.

We drive more.

Your car tires touch every street in town: past the gated mansions, through the trailer parks on the southwest side, over the two overpasses, and through the McDonald's drive-thru for ice cream and fries each night.

You tell me you're looking for the best place to be. Fireworks saturating the sky over left field. Demolition derbies a county over. Under the covers in your bed. Your foot taps an imaginary accelerator, as if the faster you move, the sooner you can get out of town. As long as you take me with you, I don't care. You hold my hand, pressing my palm onto the gear shift, and move both our arms over, backwards, until we hit the right spot. The car picks up speed, you kiss my knuckles, and my heart calms.

I don't even mind that when the stoplights flip from red to green, sometimes, not every time, but sometimes, you crush the accelerator so hard that my head bangs into my seat, and the headache spreads under my hair like a cobweb.

Go. Go. Go.

The night before you break up with me, we drive past the McDonald's, the car wash, over the creek bridge, loop through the gas station, and back towards the Wal-Mart, the abandoned Baskin Robbins, the five-screen theater with the broken marquee lights. You hold my hand on your thigh. You smell like sweat and summertime even though senior year's long-started and the leaves are turning the color of stop signs. Our lockers are right next to each other. You've already lost your biology book and I've pledged to share mine. I'm not a heart doodler, but lace patterns weave through the margins of my notes on Odysseus and Penelope.

You drive, and I'm giddy, wanting you on me in the backseat. You put my hand to your lips, kiss me under my middle knuckle, and let me go. My arm drifts to my lap. I don't understand what I don't see. I'm too busy looking out my window, my fingertips dangling in the air, drawing out our future on the horizon.

Go. Go.

Go.

# Begin Again

Four semesters of college amount to a pile of immediately-outdated text-books, scrambled German conjunctions, and three pairs of black flats, because that's what chic women wear. Butterscotch schnapps in watery hot chocolate under a loft bed the day before Christmas break. Hours of bell tolls echoing across campus to my bed as I skip Algebra 101. A lovable theater major roommate that I'll never see again after freshman year. A belly button piercing that makes me so woozy halfway through that the piercer unwraps Starbursts and pops them in my mouth for me. One rogue at-home hair dye job that turns my hair orange for two weeks. Finals. Papers. Journal pages in cramped cursive and a ton of illegally downloaded music. A new dorm, a new roommate. (This one sticks.) My first latte. Black ink smeared into clouds of gray on the side of my pinkie. Thousands of hours of carousel music at my summer job. Boys. Shy engineering majors. A fellow journalism major who knows his way around the written word, and about a dozen English majors who can do that needlessly complicated sentence dissection thing. So many farm boys; I duck a spinning lasso in the dorm lobby when I run downstairs for a pizza delivery.

So many boys.

Too many boys.

None of them are you.

Home on summer break, I walk into the movie theater — the one with the broken marquee lights — a few days before I turn 20.

I pay for my heaping bag of popcorn, turn, and see you.

I'm not the same girl, I think. I'm building a coffee palate. Mom's lace curtains are dated. I finally learned how to straighten my hair in the back.

But there you are, looking at me over a huge soda, having found mine in the sea of faces waiting for the new *Batman*, and fuck those three years and all those bell tolls. I'm seventeen and in your car, racing around town, one hand covered in kisses and the other out the window, flying.

When I summon the courage to call, which takes a few days, but not as many as it should, if we're honest, I dial your number from inside my bedroom closet. Mom crammed her extra wool sweaters into my closet while I was gone in the spring semester because I'm an ungrateful child and tell my parents every chance I get that I belong at college and I'm just home visiting. This is my mother's reminder that I'm an idiot because she's too wholesome to tell me.

You pick up. Mom's White Diamond-soaked wool crew necks might suffocate me, but the smell reminds me I'm not an idiot. Not always. "Hello. Hi. It's me."

"Hi," you say.

Almost every night, since you last kissed my hand and let it drift to my lap, I've conjured your voice up as I drift to sleep in a bed lofted six feet off the floor. Right before winter break, I realized I couldn't remember the way your tongue clicked against your teeth as you hurried through words anymore. I couldn't hear the rise and fall of your consonants, couldn't place your cadence as you whispered 'just one more kiss' before I slipped out of the car an hour past curfew. I fell asleep, my heart raw, like it was spilling onto the quilt Mom and I had so carefully picked out at Shopko the summer after you.

And with one word from you, I think: *There you are.*

But you don't know that. So, I blather about superficial shit that proves how over you I am. Schnapps in a dorm room, pierced belly button, fancy black flats, carousel music. Look at me, I've grown up, moved on, I'm like so totally mature now. I don't even remember watching your taillights fade down the street. Can't recall the crunched leaves spraying out from under your tires in your haste to leave, or what my tears tasted like as I stood frozen, wondering what to do with my hands now that yours were gone.

I sit in my closet, smothered under sweaters, and you tell me about your life now. You have a job, a good job, with health insurance, had I heard? Skipped tech school in the end. Got a tattoo. Inked barbed wire stretches around your bicep and sneaks out the bottom of your t-shirt sleeves. "You probably saw it at the movie theater," you say.

I pretend I didn't.

You cook. You have your own place. You have renter's insurance and a 401K.

And you have the whole day off. Maybe you could pick me up in an hour or so.

I pretend I'm chill, like I'm not in booty shorts and clinging to Mom's cream sweater sleeve like it's a stress ball. Like my palms aren't on fire. Like my heart isn't scaling my throat.

Dad knows who's idling in front of his house 52 minutes later, which is an impressive feat of fatherly intuition, given that you traded the apple red car in for a dirty white truck with a chipped blue racing stripe. The sun is high, and this time when the taillights disappear down the block, his daughter will be spellbound again.

My white peasant skirt swirls at my knees as I climb into the truck, and there you are. Tan. Buzzed hair. Eyes clearer than the fucking sky. You are sunshine and warm skin. Sweat and splinters. Strawberries and that time-stopping smile.

You drive. We chest puff.

"Well, I graduated with a 4.8 GPA. Honors."

"Well, I do my own taxes."

"I got placed in the advanced English courses."

"I won't have student loans."

"I outlined my first book."

"Oh yeah?" You look at me for a long moment at a stoplight. "I always knew you would."

We won't talk about high school, really, ever again, except once. You'll tell me, in a few weeks, as we lay under a plaid sheet with no clothes on, in the apartment you're about to take me to for the first time, that letting me go is your biggest regret.

You didn't know it until you cleaned out your car after graduation and found the sleeping bag in the trunk, stuffed behind a subwoofer and almost lost for good. You stood by the trunk the last night you owned it, and felt whooshing in your ears, like your equilibrium was off. Or a jet flew low overhead. Or the world was ending. Take your pick.

I loved you, you'll say. Yeah, there were other girls, but none of them mattered. Not like you.

But all of that is still a few weeks away.

Now, on this night, right before I turn twenty, I'm weary from missing you more than anything I will ever miss again. The sun's set, and I've skipped dinner. When you suggest we go to your place, I barely stop my heart from rudely exploding all over your bench seat.

Your one-bedroom is in the basement of a gigantic farmhouse-turned-apartment building. The door is next to a communal laundry space and the water heater that clunks as I take my contacts out at night. I'm certain only a heavy-duty cork board stapled to wall frames separates your bed from the washing machine. All summer, I hear people carry on conversations with their roommates as they sort laundry, and I write. I know they can hear me when you touch me in bed. I don't care.

We watch a movie. You sit on the other side of the couch, rise to grab drinks, and sit down close enough to graze my arm with your elbow.

An hour passes. The movie is about the butterfly effect. Of course it is.

I watch you drum your fingers onto your thigh like you're typing, and goosebumps raise on my skin. You ask if I'm cold, even though all the windows are open and it's still eighty degrees outside. I say no but find a way to shift my hips to you.

Ashton Kutcher dons his plot armor, and the movie keeps trucking along. I'm barely following the story, but I know exactly how your t-shirt sleeve creases against my arm. And the angle your wrist leads as you casually lift your arm and stretch it behind me on the hand-me-down floral-print couch we're stiffly perched on.

Our waters warm, Ashton keeps time traveling, and my shoulder presses against your ribcage. Your eyes are trained on the television, and I pretend like I'm watching it too. But I have to drink in this room. I have to see who you are now.

Racing paraphernalia thumbtacked to the walls. A shrine to Dale Earnhardt in red and black flags that may have been stolen from a bar we're not old enough to be in. Wal-Mart furniture, like my dorm room. A buzzing goldenrod fridge from the eighties, and a huge wooden spool that serves as a table with no chairs. Boxes of Hamburger Helper and cereal neatly line the wall next to the sink. A half-full bottle of Jack Daniels sits on top of the freezer, a badge of honor, or maybe, the bottle is just so big that it doesn't fit in any of the cupboards. Your brother's high school graduation announcement is taped to the fridge. He's long-gone to the Hills now with your mom and dad, but you're still here.

Why are you still here? The need to ask fills my throat.

Being surrounded by your things is equal parts claustrophobic and freeing. All these tangible things, but all I want to touch is you.

And you know it.

So I'm not surprised when you glance at me, and the glance becomes a look, then a study of my profile. When your hand slips to my shoulder. When you say my name. When you ask. "Can I kiss you?"

I *am* surprised I don't leap into your lap.

It's yes. Every single day.


I wake to a slamming door upstairs rattling your doorframe. Cornflower blue light streams in the window, reaching across the apartment for the far corner; I'll be awake to see that early morning sunrise a million times in my life, but it'll never be the right shade. Like the sun never quite rises the exact same way again.

We're on your couch, my head on your bicep. Your hand at my waist, warm. Heavy. My right leg hooked over your hips. Your chest rises and falls against me. My hair undone, bunched above us (hardly mermaid-like). You smell of metal, and I'll learn this is your new scent, buried in your pores, seeping out gently, sweetly, in your sleep. You stretch your legs, your belly taut as you wake and realize what's happened. You laugh. I laugh. You squeeze my hip, so light, and I'm alive again.

:::

Days start, days end, in a blur of skin and lips and sleeping in weird places at weird times. Of feeling how malleable your skin is under my fingertips. Of remembering the green specs that dot your eyes like confetti. Of French fries and whispers and country music twang floating from the tinny speakers in your bedroom window.

You drag your nail over my back one night, drawing letters and shapes, making me guess your messages. There's a heart, and my first initial, then yours. I play dumb, but roll, and kiss you so I don't black out in euphoria or implode into a zillion sparkles all over the quilt your mom made you when we were in junior high.

You're late for work more than once and get yanked into your boss's office for a minor ass chewing. I completely forget one of my shifts and rush to work in a yawny haze of frantic guilt and greasy hair. I lose time, my house key, and my watch as I slip out of my family's house, carefully patting the screen door shut with a click.

When you bring me home in the mornings, it's in the brief serenity of the crickets quieting and the sunrise breaking. You cut the engine and we roll down the street because you insist on being a gentleman, delivering me right to my door, despite the hour and my father. The dew hangs on the grass as I slip inside and up the stairs to my room like a ghost (an ecstatic, gleeful ghost); I can feel my father seething from his room, unwilling to acknowledge where I've been, and unable to talk about it. Mom corners me mid-nap late in the afternoon, and I assure that scandal and shenanigans will not occur.

But I want them to.

So, two days after I turn twenty, three years after you asked me on a date to the fireworks, six months after I realized I forgot what your voice sounds like, two weeks after the movie theater lobby, and eight days after I called you under an almost-avalanche of wool sweaters, with a five-hour old hickey deepening to plum peeking out of my bra and a heart that's in true danger of actually exploding, I send you a text.

*I'm ready.*

*U sure? We can wait.*

*I trust you.*

And lord, do I ever.

:::

Summer is rude, and flirts with ending too soon. We feel it before it starts, the wind down, but it only makes us ramp up. We're always together. Staying in bed until noon. Huddling in the truck before I lead you into my house for your first family Sunday pot roast. (Dad glares but behaves. Mom preens, happy you're finally eating her roast after all these years.) You don't smoke around me, and I get braver with your friends. You kiss my knuckles as you drive. Sunshine moves over your face as we turn a corner one afternoon, and I can't look away. You are everything. You always have been.

Too quickly — the last night of the summer: the county fair.

We stand in a gravel lot in front of a concert stage. A girl in too-big black cowboy boots, with massive hair that spirals to her waist and a sparkly halter dress, strums the shit out of her guitar. She sings about her lost love, and how she hopes when he hears Tim McGraw, he thinks of her. The air is sweet with hoppy beer and sugary funnel cakes. Behind us, the Ferris wheel's lights blink red, blue, yellow, drifting around and around, the baskets cradling people as it lifts to the clouds and returns riders to the earth again. And you're right beside me for all of it.

There isn't anything more I will ever want, I am certain.

Last night, you told me you love me (again) for the first time (again).

I'd spent the day schlepping slushies to preschoolers and testy parents under hot sunshine. At your place, I climbed over you as you separated clean laundry on the coffee table. A neat pile of your Sturgis Rally t-shirts, mixed in with one of my creamy yellow work polos. Your white socks knotted together, and a couple of my cozy cotton shorts I'd stashed there for sleeping. You let me nestle my toes under your ass as you folded, and the repetition, the reliability, the comfort of it lulled me to sleep.

I stirred when you flung my arm around your neck to carry me to bed. You smelled like nighttime: evergreen body wash and nicotine masked by toothpaste as you tucked me in with my favorite blanket in your bed. "I have a secret," you whispered, nestling the blanket around my waist.

The living room light tiptoed in, filling your bedroom with warm, brown shadows. You'd already taken my glasses and put them on the headboard, and looking at you through sleepy, near-sighted eyes, with the watercolor of golden light behind you, is a memory I'll hold onto until my dying day. "I must know."

"I love you," you said. "In the big way."

I know. It quit being a secret when we were seventeen, and maybe even before that.

I try to tell you that I love you too, but it gets lost as you kiss me back to sleep.

At the concert, a beer cup dangles from your fingertips. The rogue beer bracelet, borrowed from a twenty-one-year-old friend and hastily fastened to your wrist with scotch tape I grabbed on my way out, threatens to unstick. I take the cup and sip. The girl on stage is still singing. *Someday you'll turn your radio on. I hope it takes you back to that place.*

"It'll be dark enough for the fireworks soon," I say, handing you the beer.

The sky turns navy, then black. We mingle with our friends, stepping apart to discuss the finer points of sneaking into the beer tent (you) and comparing tans and how we wish somebody would just grab a hard lemonade instead of beer (me), but we watch each other through the maze of bodies, plotting, circling, waiting until the peanut gallery won't notice that we're opposite-poled magnets and pulling to each other no matter what.

When the golden sparkles erupt in the sky, you pull me to you for good. You set your chin where my neck curves to my shoulder and our hands tangle over my belly button. We both look up. Always looking up.

I crane my neck to watch each firework turn your face different colors until it fades and the next bursts over us, and I get lost trying to figure out how I'll ever write this moment with any clarity. It's not possible. This is too still, too perfect, to ever be muddied by my clumsy prose.

"I love you," I whisper, my words landing in your ear.

You kiss my cheek, lingering, and your eyelashes brush my skin.

"I love you more," you say.

:::

12:03 am. That's our nightly appointment. The calendar flips to the next day, but my night only starts when your voice is larger than life in my flip Nokia. I'm always ready. Studying done, pajamas on, teeth brushed. Mascara crumbled into cotton balls in the garbage, contacts floating in solution, and I'm watching the seconds tick by in my twin bed in a bedroom the size of a large closet in my college apartment, waiting for you to hurry and clock out already. Every single night, we fall asleep together, our phones tucked against pillows, one hundred and fifty-one miles apart

"Hi baby girl," you say, "hang on." You hustle to your truck, yelling rude expletives to your coworkers, and everyone cackles. I hear your boots crunch over gravel, the truck door squawk open. Your grunt as you bounce in behind the wheel and fasten your seatbelt because I gave you enough hell all summer to be safe. The engine roars, and you peel out as much as you can on gravel as you get the hell out of dodge. Every single night.

You speed down the highway under the stars and fill me in on shit our friends get into or complain about how some machine I don't understand the function of always busts when you're in a hurry. I tamp down burning jealousy of whoever gets to see you through the McDonald's drive-thru window. French fries in the passenger seat and homebound, I hear you bang your closed fist on the steering wheel and know the straw is trapped in your clutch and you're ripping it open. I tell you my Media Law class is fascinating and simultaneously kicking my ass, or my roommate and her boyfriend won't stop dry humping against the kitchen sink, and I walked in on them again. Every single night.

I dash home on Fridays in the same way settlers tore from the coasts during the gold rush. I struggle — try — want — so much to be present at school, and not let my mind wander to you, but you're too far away. You're the light in the dark, and I'm the mosquito buzzing right to it. And buzz, I do.

Fall weekends mean movie dates and bonfires, our numb asses perched on coolers we spring up from when someone needs a beer. Winter sinks over us, and I love you even more in the snow. Snowflakes get stuck in your dark hair, and I study how each flake cuts and zags within its frozen self before it melts and becomes part of you. In the coldest spells, we run to the truck and you throw open the driver's door and you all but throw me in, and slide in after. Your lips are frozen, and you take my hands and blow onto my skin as we wait for the truck to blast hot, dry air onto our faces. Saturdays and Sundays are for extended, cozy afternoon naps, huddled under quilts, and so much sex to make up for when I'm gone during the week.

I don't head back to school until sunrise on Monday mornings, but I feel the longing of missing you already on Sundays. It eats away at me, driving my old friends, those damned buzzing bees, to flare again, but now they're frantic — trying to pack as much of you into my life, onto my skin, as I can in two days a week.

The buzzing leaks from me sometimes. I slip, and let you see how my heart keeps splintering away in chunks as I drive out of town and go back to school. How when I leave campus to come home, I know I'm giving up parts of college I dreamed about when we were in our in-between: my friends and crowding into bathrooms to do each other's hair and sip strawberry margs from glasses the same color as the highlighters we use in our textbooks. Football games and library study sessions and movie nights with seven people crammed on a loveseat when no one can hear the TV because no one will shut up.

You spend those anxious, sad nights tracing stars on the inside of my hands to root me again, here, with you.

In the spring, we visit every lake in a twenty-mile radius. We borrow your friend's boat, or crawl down the incline next to a bridge, and sit on the cement in the weak sunshine. You fish, wiggling minnows onto your hook.

I watch your fingers work and want to press the inside of your wrists to my lips. Instead, I pull my book from your tackle box or watch the leaves begin to grow on the trees around the lake again and understand what it means for those leaves to unravel in graceful, higher air.

But I treasure our phone calls. Everyone we know is asleep. I don't feel stretched too thin, or as if I'm missing out on something, somewhere. It's just me and you. Cornflower blue.

One Thursday in April, flies hum as they weave around the ditch weed on the road from campus to my apartment. It sounds like summer, and the sunshine burning the back of my hands through the windshield feels like you, and I need to see you. I text you as soon as I park. *Big surprise. You'll get it tomorrow before work.*

The rest of the afternoon and through your shift, my phone lights up consistently, as if wearing me down will make me spill.

"I hate surprises; you know that." It's 12:04. Your tires spit up gravel as you leave the parking lot. I hear the roar like a helicopter took up residence on your hood. "Tell me."

"That, my dear, is the exact opposite of a surprise." My phone is jammed between my shoulder and ear as I dump clean laundry onto my bed. I pull out a t-shirt and toss it in my overnight bag without folding it.

"Can I guess?"

I smile, and shake out my favorite yoga pants. "I'll allow it."

"Does it fly?"

"Uh, no."

"Can I…" You funnel oxygen into your lungs. I can picture your gaze leaping all over the dark road in thought, and not paying attention to driving. Here's hoping no curbs jump out. "Can I eat it?"

"I'd prefer you not."

"Can I show it to my friends?"

"One would suppose you could."

You figure me out; I know it by your sigh. It's the smallest thing, this little tuft of air that lifts, and sinks into a low hum. It's gritty, and sexy as hell, and sweet, because I'm the only person in the world who gets to know the difference.

The sigh, then: "Can I keep it forever?"

"Yes," I say. Forever, and ever and ever.

A long beat. The quietest of sweet sighs. "Cool."

:::

Sometimes we cross wires, but who doesn't?

I have a year of my undergrad left. Your dad wants you to move to the Black Hills. Your mom and brother are happy there, living a town over from your dad. You're only staying here because of me. You're not meant for East River.

I find myself stumbling into communication blocks. For being a writer, words shouldn't be this stiff. This difficult to craft into something that will resonate in my brain, and in your heart. I grow frozen by the fear of missing out. Missing you. Missing the life I was slowly constructing for myself, when I thought you didn't want me. The words I crave are nearly in reach, but get stuck in my throat, or tangled at the tips of my fingers.

For all my charades and all your tangible life skills, we aren't the people we'll grow to be, not yet, and that knowledge churns like the tires on my car when I run home to you. As I drive hours upon hours, I try to weave our pieces together, clinging to what matters, filtering out what doesn't. I don't know how to fully braid you into my life, and me into yours, when our predestined futures look so incredibly different.

Again with the tropes that work so well in books but never in real life. The mechanic and the writer. The camo-clad hunter and the might-as-well-be-a vegetarian. The good ol' boy and...me.

And let's face it: we don't have role models to emulate our situation in real life. My parents are so traditional it hurts, and are, in a lot of ways, almost the same person. (You and I are not.) Your parents are friendly but weren't right together. (You and I are.)

That leaves us to our own devices. Claire and Bender probably don't last a week after the Breakfast Club disbands. Lainey, post-credits, is still pissed Zach bet on her with Paul Walker, and it's over before it starts. Don't even get me started with Drew Barrymore kissing her teacher on the pitcher's mound.

This is up to us to figure out.

We don't know what we're doing. Or how to do it.

But you're what I want. More than a college degree, more than making Dad happy, more than figuring out what the fuck to do with a journalism degree when all I want to do is write books. My biggest dream came true. It was you. It was always you.

The rest was just noise.

Well. I wish the rest was just noise. But its whispers, its murmurs, keep growing, blooming. And you hear it too.

:::

I pay three months of rent so I have a room in the fall, leave textbooks scattered on my bed, and move in with you for real for the summer. We've made it a year. You still trace letters on my shoulders, and I drift to sleep to you drawing stars falling over our initials. We go to the Hills to visit your family. Your eyes are bright as we hike to a stream near your dad's house, and I know having you close is on borrowed time. I look around the meandering forest, take deep breaths, and think about how I could live out here with you, under these trees.

We come home, see county fair concerts, sit at bonfires, hit our fishing spots, don't always hold hands in the truck, and sometimes, I go to bed before you get home from work at night. When you aren't home, I sit on the futon cross-legged and try to turn us into words. Something to define the lingering fear of you leaving again, of me gaining independence from the clinging anxiety. I need you to call us what I want us to be, rather than what I'm terrified we are.

But trying to write our story before we've lived it is impossible. The words fail me. And anyway I've always, always looked to you to define what I can't.

So I claw at what I do know.

"We aren't settling," I say one morning. You woke up grumpy and I'm taking my feelings out on a blueberry muffin mix with a wooden spatula over the oven. You're messily spooning Fruity Pebbles from a bowl to your face. The August humidity permeates the basement; the walls are gleaming, damp. I can't breathe. I want to drop the muffin batter into the sink and run.

I keep talking instead. Because even when the words fail, the chatter never ends. "We're just settling into us. That's what's supposed to happen."

You nod, and barely part your lips to slurp the milk from the bowl.

The ending begins as you help me pack my car two days before the fall semester. You hand me my hamper of clothes. When the handles twist and tangle our fingers together, neither of us laugh. We shake ourselves free and move on.

I ask you to visit for a weekend in September. It's time you get to know my life there. See the other parts of my life that I love. But instead of ready agreement, or even eye contact, you look across the street into the streaky sunshine. Everything is burnt by the sun at the end of the summer; it hasn't rained in days, and the green is gone. I turn to look where you're staring, but only see the hot haze weaving in the air. The tree branches droop, as if they're repelling another late afternoon of hot sunshine that's just out to kill it. You shake your head, and shove your hands in your jeans, and drop a chaste kiss on my cheek. "I can't, my dear."

And I let that be okay.

I go out with my friends instead. We sip strawberry margs and crowd in the bathroom curling each other's hair and slicking on lip gloss. At the bars, boys buy me drinks, and I thank them, but slide the glasses to whichever friend has an empty cup.

Our midnight calls never stop, but they grow short, terse. Sleepy 'love you mores' turn into wide awake 'k, good night thens'.

Years later, you tell me you didn't realize how I only had two semesters left, and thought I was set on grad school. I tell you I would have moved to the Hills after graduation. I would have lived under those trees with you, blocks from your dad or down the street from your mom. Filled our living room with books and not thought twice about the white-tail head mounted opposite the patio door.

I would've gone anywhere you wanted. If you'd asked.

But you never did.

:::

On a meaningless Monday in October, you call at 10 pm.

I'm crying before I pick up.

It was cruel, using our phone calls to make the final cut. It wasn't like the red car lights disappearing down my street in high school. No, no, my dear. It was dismantling the future I *wanted*. That you said you wanted too.

It was letting go of — no — pushing away memories that hadn't happened yet. Laughs that will never bubble from our stomachs. Keys to our home that won't jingle against my knee as I drive to work. Casual pictures never snapped on shitty cell phone cameras next to bonfires. Photos from our wedding that will never happen, never be framed, and never be hung on your mom's wall next to your senior picture. Babies with your eyes and my hair we'll never rock to sleep. I won't watch my hand grow smaller and wrinkled inside yours as our cornflower mornings pass by quicker than we can ever understand.

It was you, running. Again.

You hang up first.

# The State Motel

College graduation comes. Goes. The economy is shit, and I'm lucky to find a low-paying office job back in our hometown. But I can't hack it. Don't want to hack it. You're long gone now; rumor and Facebook tell me you waited a month and moved to your family. I don't blame you. But I can't live at home without you.

I move back to my college town. My friends are here. My new boy is here.

He isn't you.

I hustle and keep my head down. A serving gig leads to a job in marketing at the university.

Time moves on in campus bell tolls and pauses at stoplights. My new boy sticks around, years pass, and he stops being new. We're not good for each other, but restlessness fills the space in my heart you vacated, and being wanted by anyone is better than feeling my mind wander to you. It's easier to smile, to flirt, (and admittedly way more fun) to prance around in sky high heels and jeans that make my ass look entirely fabulous. Hot Girl is an easy role to slip into. It's effortless. And the attention distracts me, which is the goal anyway.

My boy and I break up, and I try to feel hurt, or sadness, or anything really, but all the nerve endings you lit up like the Fourth of July are still singed, and I don't know how to feel anything at all.

But I keep writing about you. Us. Trying to define, turn the muddy clear. There's truth in all these pages, somewhere, I think, as I parse through years' worth of cramped handwritten journals and notes, and more open documents on my laptop than what's healthy.

I keep looking for us in the space between the words. To capture how real we were, because if I can't, maybe we never were. I also want to be new, mature, wiser, but all I am is weary. The hopeful girl on my parents' living room floor, basking in sunshine under lace curtains, doesn't recognize me. And I ask her to turn around, so she can't shatter this shell, and make me heal already. I'm not ready. I don't know if I'll ever be ready.

None of this is reason to call you. You have a newborn daughter and an ex making your life difficult. I can't make your life easier. Those days are gone.

Like that ever stopped me.

As the phone rings on your end, the bell tolls on campus: twelve slow melodic rings in the night. Schnapps in a dorm room, mascara crumbled into cotton balls, White Diamonds, carousel music. Blank ink smeared into clouds of gray on the side of my pinkie.

"Hello?"

I say: "Hey. It's me."

I mean: I miss you. I can't be alone one more night, and I probably still love you. Talk me through this, please? Please.

You sigh. The lift, the hum.

"It's twelve-oh-one," you say. "You're early."

You don't have to talk me through this.

I still love you.

Fuck.

:::

You don't work nights anymore, and I have work early, so our phone calls shift to 9 pm, exactly. You call me as you boil noodles for your late dinners. I call you after a bad date that I bail on early — the dude smelled like patchouli and when I walked into his apartment, every surface was covered in tiny, lit tea candles. A bong sat prominently on the coffee table, both blocking my view of the truly terrible Matt Damon movie, and sort of... daring me to either imbibe or run.

You gasp in faux horror. "What would your dad say?"

I snort. "He'd probably be more concerned about the clear fire hazard. I was sure I was gonna light myself on fire."

"Well, you've always been kind of a klutz."

Another night, you tell me about your baby girl. Her momma has only let you visit once. It's a pool of heartache I have no right wading into.

Naturally, I do.

"She has your eyes," I say, looking at the picture you sent me. I'm in bed, feet on my wall under my poster print of Starry Night that I've tacked up in two dorm rooms and three apartments in two cities. Your girl's eyes are shaped like yours; the corners turn down slightly, like teardrops, and are round right in the middle, perfect circles. Yours gleam in mischief; hers will too.

Blankets rustle, and you exhale like you sat up in a hurry. "I want to see you. I can't go far, and I know you don't want to drive all the way here, but I looked... Pierre is a good halfway point."

My bedroom spins. This was what I wanted. Why I'd called, right?

And the next weekend is a long one: Memorial Day. The start of the summer.

Like there was even a question.

:::

The highway is full of holiday traffic on its way to the river. Sticky wind swirls through my wide-open window, ruining my hair and the map I surreptitiously printed in color at the communal printer in my office. I take deep breaths. Fill the old, creaky parts of me with oxygen so I don't pass out and crash my car into some poor farmer's ditch.

I hope you won't notice how empty I am. And when you see me, the real me, because you will, I hope you're okay with the missing, phantom parts of me now.

In town, my stomach seizes every time I pass a car with a man driving. That's obviously not uncommon, so you can imagine how twisted my guts are, hoarding bile produced via anxiety. You're here in this town, somewhere. Not on paper, not my version of you recreated through my lens, but...you.

The bees wake.

You beat me to the hotel. Your car is a small black sedan, void of candy wrappers and printed MapQuest directions. It's so practical. Time clicked along, and you kept growing into the man I knew you would be when we were kids.

Why did I spend more time picturing — and believing in — your future than I did mine?

You wave, awkwardly, like you practiced in the rearview mirror the entire drive over, and when the big moment arrived, you fucked it all up. Your hair is beginning to recede in peaks above each eyebrow, like your dad's did when we were in middle school.

But your smile is perfect. Will always be perfect. Warm as sunshine.

We meet in front of your car. You open your arms. I zag, you do too, and our heads nearly collide. The air is clammy, and the insides of my elbows stick together. Wind whips up goosebumps on my arms. My black sundress, dotted in tiny red flowers, is suddenly too short, too young. It billows like a hot air balloon, exposing my underwear between our cars. I yank the hem down.

You watch me press my palms down my thighs, as I long for the cardigan in my bag. "It's good to see you," you say. "Really good."

I look up from the poppies. Your lips curve into a smirk; you're dying to make an underwear joke. Probably make underwear into a plural, or remind me you've seen it all before. That's not the point — not even close to the blunt side of the point — but my heart settles. And I want to touch your face. Feel you lean into me. Make sure you're real. You're real, right?

"You too," I manage, instead.

"Should we...?" You nod to a cracked screen door featuring a black plate with dirty letters that say Office superglued inside the glass. I follow, you hold the door open, and the inside of the lobby matches its vaguely horror-movie inspired entry. Lime green, dirt-coated carpet. Wood paneled walls. A tiny tube TV on a rickety bookshelf by the door. The Weather Channel broadcasts the forecast every ten minutes.

You smack the bell on the desk, and shrug as if to say, "It's the best we can do." I'm barely making over minimum wage. You have a baby. We both need gas money to get home.

As you check us in, the guy behind the front desk watches me, his eyes lingering at my hips. I wish again for a sweater. In an attempt to hide, I step to the window, looking for the river from the hill the motel sits on, but only see more of the depressing motel. Our cars are in the middle of the parking lot, the U-shaped rows of rooms wrapping around it, like a snake in its last maneuvers before the kill. Outdoor entrances to every room. Rod iron gates and concrete stairs. Pitiful white geraniums in chipped pots by the front door. A Coke machine across the parking lot sends out an SOS in blinks, bulbs about to go out.

I want to run. Even with you signing away two nights of a hotel fee, I almost slip out the door. Where would I go? Not my apartment. Not yours. Maybe north. Maybe our hometown. The opportunities are endless. The opportunities are non-existent.

You click the pen, sign your name.

Behind you, lace curtains flutter above a rattling fan from Wal-Mart. They aren't delicate like Mom's and have never been real white, but they're lace.

And I see us at seventeen. On my living room floor. Your hand cradles mine. My cocker spaniel grunts in his sleep. I forgot to vacuum. Pretty shadows dance over your lips that I desperately press against mine as soon as I realize I can kiss you back. Nothing will ever be the same again.

You hand me our room key. I take it.

The AC wheezes to life as I thumb around to find the right setting of knobs to cool our room. Dust sputters out the top. I flip the bedside lamp on. The peach light barely helps.

You drop your duffel and my overnight bag in the chair next to the door, getting your first eyeful of the room. "Shit."

I straighten up, my hands on my hips, taking it in too. More wood-paneled walls. Heavy forest green curtains above the air conditioner. Highlighter green and neon pink nylon comforters that had probably never seen better days. Four pillows that may still feature yesterday's tenant's skull dents.

You laugh. "Remember when we stayed at that Super 8 for your cousin's wedding? Your dad was so pissed you slept in my room."

"What would my aunts think?" I imitate Dad, my tone snobby. "If only the aunts could see us now."

You scratch your head. "I'm glad no one knows I'm here."

I cross my arms and dig in my bag for my cardigan. This fucking cardigan. I need it.

"You know what I mean." I feel you reach for my elbow. My arm hair spikes as you pull back.

I'm alight.

So that's still a thing.

Common sense, bless her, elbows lust out of the way and reports that my long-desired cardigan is touching my fingertips. I pull my sweater over my shoulders. "No, I know," I say. "Me too." I finger-comb my hair behind my ears. "Should we get dinner?"

We drive down the main drag, find a McDonald's, and decide to get ice cream tomorrow. We land at a greasy spoon truck stop on the opposite edge of town. You try, it seems, to get us as far away from our motel as possible.

We sit, we order, and we stare at each other over filmy water glasses and a pair of salt and pepper shakers. I could ask how your baby girl is. How you managed to knock up a batshit crazy eighteen-year-old (don't you remember us at eighteen?! We barely walked upright.) You could ask why I was hung up on a jackass who drank so much I spent nights waiting for the county jail to call to bail his ass out, but you don't. We're candid on the phone. But phone calls mean distance, and distance means ambiguity. None of this is real, why we're here, until I listen to the fluorescent lights above us buzz.

I'm debating asking if you know why all truck stop salt shaker lids have pepper sprinkled around the salt holes, as if it's a secret conspiracy no one let me in on, when you rescue me from myself and speak. Finally.

"I was relieved you called." You fold your hands on the table. Your cuticles are ragged. I picture you in a waiting room at a nondescript hospital, picking, slicing your way through that translucent skin with your dull thumb nail, digging down to the white half-moon on each finger, waiting for word on your daughter. She'd been a few weeks early.

You open your palms to me. I slide my hands over yours, next to the tiny bowl of creamers.

"I think of you all the time." Your eyes focus on my fingertips pressing your wrists. (You are here, I think, watching my fingerprints indent your skin. Look at that.) "When I moved, I found a hundred of your bobby pins in the carpet, in my drawers, under the bathroom sink. And a couple earrings behind the headboard."

"They were cheap," I say. "You could have tossed them."

"And your cross-country shirt." You continue, as if I didn't speak. As if you need to tell me all the things I left behind. "The one from seventh grade when you only ran that one season, so you wore it to bed instead."

I can't picture the t-shirt. Even a little.

"It was white, with blue letters. A girl running with a giant eagle head behind her." Your fingers trace the air across your chest, drawing a serif font for a forgotten t-shirt. "Doesn't matter."

I grip your wrist to stop you from bounding out of this restaurant, because you have a habit of running. And I want to feel your pulse. The pattern of your heartbeat is too tempting, even if I'm about to roast you alive. "Sounds like you did a shitty job packing all my stuff up when you dumped me."

Your laugh explodes like a bomb and fades just as quickly. You turn my wrist over and trace the blue veins that pump blood to my hands. "I kept it all. Everything I missed, I kept. In case."

I picture hundreds of bobby pins tangled, rusted in a sandwich bag in a drawer. "You didn't have to."

You shrug. "They were yours."

When I write, words jumble in my brain over my left eyebrow, jostling for space on the page. They're like a memory I'm yet to have, and the words race down my arms and out my fingers like sparks, sometimes even before I know what they are. I'm almost never at a loss for words.

But I don't know what to say now.

The server brings your cheeseburger and my house salad. We split your fries. I pick the onions off my iceberg and let the purple rings rest on my napkin, the damp circles soaking through the paper. We eat, and the talking fades again.


We're back at the motel.

I drop my purse on the bed. You flip on the peach lamp.

Somehow, we're pressing against each other. In the car, it'd been a herculean feat to not grab your fingers and twist them within mine. I'd been so focused on the whereabouts of your hands the entire drive, and how your arm hair trailed to an end above your thumb, and your decimated cuticles, and how your knuckles are still rocky knots that do things to me that I noticed every, single time your pinky twitches in my direction. But now, in our peach-lit, wood-paneled room, you're nervous. You won't meet my eye, even as your knuckles trail down my arms to my wrists, and I fight the shivers.

"This is a foregone conclusion, isn't it?" It's not a question, but I make it sound like one.

You step back. "You know it doesn't have to be."

I close the space you gave us (how many times have I done that now?) and roll your t-shirt sleeve up to trace your barbed wire tattoo circling your bicep. How many times had I skimmed my nail over the ink out of boredom, as you swatted me away because it tickled? Held it as you were over me in bed, kissing the skin it covers as you grabbed the headboard as you came? Leaned my head against it as we watched late night movies, or the landscape pass on long drives, or boats sway gently away on the lake from our fishing spot on cold spring Sundays?

"I want it to be," I say. "I want you."

Parking lot lights peek around the curtains. My chest fills with memories of other curtains, other walls, other dingy bedrooms that had been ours.

Your beard tickles when we meet in the middle. It's muscle memory, how you make my guts turn to mush. You kiss my forehead, my eyelids, my cheek bones, the tip of my nose.

"Can I kiss you?" you ask.

Yes. Every single day.

After, we share the shower and giggle over the short shower head. Soapy water polka dots the floor as you grab a washcloth from the shelf over the toilet so I can dry my face. My chest aches. You remember I hate water dripping from my eyelashes to my cheeks.

We kiss again, and then I don't care anymore about water on my face. You grow hard in my hands, and with a twitch of my eyebrow, and your shit-eating grin, you slip between my legs, one hand on the bottom of my spine, the other flat-palming the shower tiles to keep us upright. I come faster than I ever have in my life, my face in your neck. Freckles crowd your shoulder like a constellation. I'd forgotten.

You have the grace to wait until I'm toweling off my legs. "I still got it, huh?"

I ball up my towel and chuck it at you, instantly regretting it as it puffs to the floor like a cloud. You toss me yours and leave the bathroom naked to dig through your bag for shorts, laughing.

In bed, I kiss you, fast, like we'd never stopped. You pull me against your chest, and I swear your exhale could send a rocket to space. "I'm so glad you're here." Your chin brushes my forehead, and it feels nice.

You fall asleep quickly, but sleep won't take me. Is it that you still have the weird tuft of white chest hair just north of your pec? Is it the strange headlights peeking in and swiping between the television antennas on the other side of the room? Is it that when you kiss me, you still — still — cup the back of my head, as if I'm the flight risk?

And maybe I am. Because all I see is your car running out of streetlights on the county highway. A sleeping bag flat in weeds, and unvacuumed floors. Tatted, delicate shadows of lace sweeping over cheeks, and wool turtlenecks and Media Law binders and peppermint schnapps and shifty cocker spaniels. Scotch-tape grabbing wrist hair at the fair, hoppy beer, a girl in too-big cowboy boots. Twisted laundry basket handles and midnight phone rings and a Hot Girl persona, and carousel music and quilts picked out at Shopko while my heart attempts to vacate my body every morning as my eyes flutter open.

When the threat of life without you is as real as you are, I do the only thing to temper my panic. I count.

My head on your arm, my hair splayed across the pillow. My hand over your chest, skimming the skin over your heart. My knee curved over your belly. Your arm cranked behind my neck, the back of your fingers tangled in my split ends. In your sleep, you take a deep breath, shift, and kiss my head.

I stare at the wood panels as you sleep in my arms.

*I think of you all the time.*

*Everything I missed, I kept. In case.*

*I'm so glad you're here.*

I see you collecting penny hair pins on your dresser as you fill boxes, eventually cupping and sweeping the pile into a sandwich bag. In your mom's driveway behind your car, clinging to the sleeping bag like a life preserver, and remembering starlight that looked like glitter in the snow after a blizzard. The light that journeyed an eternity only to find our patch of grass empty. No smiles to catch, no one to applaud its beauty, as it ceases to exist.

I always thought I missed you the most.

I was wrong. You'd been telling me all along: you loved me more.

You do.

And I shouldn't be here.

:::

When you wake, your lips sweep my forehead before your eyes open. You go to brush your teeth, and the shower blasts on. I rise and pull another sundress from my bag. This one is suddenly too short too; it'd been fine at home. I slip my cardigan on. The shower turns off, and I pull my hair into a bun to busy my fingers from grinding my knuckles to dust.

You come out and drop the towel to the floor as you dress. I look away. "What should we do today?"

"I don't know what to do here."

Your smile is naughty and warm and wedges into the spaces between my ribs, and for a second, I feel better.

"I can think of things we can do," you murmur, crossing the room. You move hair from my neck and your lips on my skin make me sink into your grip. My body and my heart react in the predictable stutter-step that's stopped time since we were seventeen.

I press into your body; this makes sense. Not wanting to be here is petrifying. It makes every decision I've ever made off-kilter at best, wicked at worst. So, I kiss you hard, my arms wound around your neck. You turn to putty wherever my fingers go. My skirt is balled in your fists, and the familiar pings of want bubble under my belly button and creep down. I feel like I'm in high school, crawling around in your backseat as we figure out how to mess around without conking our heads. We're twenty, three am, perched on the kitchen counter in our underwear. You're between my legs as we trade the spoon, hunting for the chocolate ribbons, the rest of the ice cream melting in the bucket.

:::

In the end, we sit on the riverbank. It's too hot for my cardigan, but the heavy wool keeps my dress from drifting up, so I keep it on.

"Just take it off," you say, watching me fidget.

I try to joke. "I did that already."

You look to the river as the water crashes by. Montana got too much snow this winter, and now with the fast thaw, people too close to the dam — us — wait for major flooding. We're sitting too close, right in the floodplain, only a few yards to the river. But no one's yelled at us yet.

You kiss my cheek and work your way to my neck. Once a welcome respite in a world full of carousel music and childishly-penned essays about you, your beard scratches me now. My skin is tight.

I spring up. "Let's walk." I offer my hand, and you weave our fingers together, but you watch me, finally actually the flight risk. I take a deep breath and cough on mist from the crashing river.

You bring our clasped hands to your lips and kiss my third knuckle.

The bees don't calm. But at least they quit attempting escape.

We walk forever. Down the bike path, weave along the river, and turn when the path curves back into town. We walk past where we started, and we shield our eyes when we aren't under leaves. At a vantage point, a deck built into the banks, I pull you next to the fence to look down. The river spurs furiously underneath us, past the bluffs and to the southeast.

"You'll tell me, when you can, won't you?" Your chin lands on my shoulder as we look to the same horizon.

I nod. Your shoulders relax, like you'd been holding your breath.

"Promise."

"I promise."

Our fingers thread together over the fence, with nothing under them but space and water. I count.

Your forehead on the back of my shoulder now, looking to the top of your sneakers. Our fingers overlap in a million places. Our wrists curve together like spoons. Your chest grazes my spine as I look over the river. Lace curtains drift, like the windows are breathing. Your knees tap under the dinner table as Mom serves Sunday pot roast. Books in your tackle box. I love you in the big way. Sunshine moves over your face and I can't look away.

Red taillights become dots, then specks, then nothing. Three garbage bags inside your apartment door, full of my clothes and books. Keys from our first house. Wedding photos on walls. Babies we'll never rock to sleep. Thisisdone. Weareover. Icantdothisanymore.

I am always going to want to kiss you.

I love you more.

Can I keep it forever, you'd asked.

No.

:::

After dark, we each sit on a bed and pass the McDonald's bag back and forth. Empty French fry boxes, beer bottles, and napkins creased with grease litter the table under the peach lamp. *Rock of Love* plays on mute and we laugh about a mishap with a sparkler bomb and a bird one Fourth of July. About when you turned 21 and I somehow got you down the stairs to bed without killing either of us. About when I turned 21, and you threw me over your shoulder without breaking a sweat.

Your laughs fade. I tug at my hair. The air changes, and your brown eyes have gone sad. All of our memories, just that. And here we are now, still in the moment, as it fades to memory.

"After I heard you moved, I went back to the apartment," I blurt.

"Why?" You set your empty beer bottle on the end table.

I shrug. "Did the tour of Aberdeen. Went back to the lake. Took the route from my house to your apartment."

"What were you looking for?"

I finish my beer and set the bottle next to yours. "I think maybe you. Any sign that you and I had been there, together."

You open your mouth. I hold up my hand.

"You felt like the beginning of something massive," I say. "Each time you feel like that, and if I let myself, you would feel like that today, here, now." My eyes go foggy. "And I'd sit and wait for you forever. I was certain I couldn't live, couldn't breathe, write, exist without you. You were — are — in every piece of me, still."

You bow your head.

"You sat next to me every night and kissed me like you'd kiss me forever, and I was so fucking happy," I whisper. "Then you'd ask if I was hungry or tell me about your day, those little things, the everyday of it all — it was all I ever wanted." You look at me. "You were all I ever wanted."

Your eyes shine in the lamplight, and if I could bottle that glint, that sparkle, and carry it with me always, I would. My god, I would.

"I wanted to ask you to marry me," you whisper.

And I can see it, our life. I own camo I never wear and begrudgingly accept your blue jeans on our wedding day. Our kids bow hunt and write complex sentences worthy of the Oxford comma. You hang your white-tail head trophy next to the bookcases in the living room chock full of celebrity memoirs and young adult literature and books about feminism. I ask for Taylor Swift on repeat in the truck, and you tilt your eyes to the ceiling like she's the worst, but you sing every word under your breath. Especially her happy songs. We eat homemade chislic at least once a week, and you don't shake me off when I pat down your sleeve when it rolls up your bicep as you wash the dishes. You wolf whistle when I cut all my hair off and dye what's left a delicate rose gold, and I jump onto your tailgate and trade stories with your dad and our friends in the backyard at the fire pit. Our babies grow, know their purposes, and find their versions of you. All the sunscreen in the world won't stop my laugh lines, and your old man hand is my favorite thing I'll ever see curled inside my wrinkly fingers.

Our love was real. Holy shit, was it ever.

"I would have said yes." Every single day, until all the stars burned out.

"I'm always going to want you." Your voice is soft as you dig your thumb into the middle of your palm. "Always will."

I move to sit next to you on our bed, the one we'd slept in last night, the bed we'll share tonight. We'll sleep fitfully. I'll wake in the dark and feel the bed cold and reach for you and you'll already be rolling to me. You'll tuck a chunk of hair behind my ear with way too much precision to suggest you've slept at all. I'll hook my leg over your hip and burrow my face into the soft flesh under your collarbone. And we'll wait for the sun to rise.

You put your hand on my thigh and weave our fingers together. I can't tell you how relieved I am, how the bees have finally stilled, and how a sliver of true honesty was all it took. Words float above my left eyebrow, organizing into something thoughtful, something eloquent. Something that matters. I close my eyes, and lean against your shoulder, pretending I'm writing this moment into reality. The words will be true to us. And when they materialize, I'm not surprised by what they are.

"I love you," I say.

You don't seem surprised either. "I love you more."

:::

It's Tuesday morning. The day after Memorial Day. We sit at a four-top in the IHOP, decked out in Americana for the holiday. You smile at me over your pile of pancakes. That smile. Your crooked incisor, whiskers curling at your lip. Dimples for days. Your smile is the warmest thing I will ever, I think then, find in this world.

A strawberry slides off the melting whip on my waffle. "I'll pay you for half the motel."

"No." My strawberry plunks to my plate when you shake your head. "I want to take care of it."

Under the table, your boot finds my bare ankle. You nudge my feet between yours; my toes nestle under the bottom of your jeans.

"Okay."

You drive me back to our motel for my car. You're going west to your daughter, and I'm going east to whatever waits for me. The car is hot as we weave through the unfamiliar roads for the last time. We keep our windows up.

At the motel, you park next to my car. These moments aren't new, not to us. In high school, your car idled next to the curb, staring down a road I didn't get to go down with you. In college, you called me from the couch where I dreamed my big dreams, knowing I'd race home in the dark, and find nothing but garbage bags full of my clothes.

But I get it, now. Why you left the car running. Why you called after you packed my stuff. The escape route was key; without it already in play, you wouldn't leave.

This whole time, I've been paging through my journals and tracing our steps through our hometown, looking for the ghosts of us. Of you. But if we were so incandescent that the starlight couldn't find us again, how was I supposed to?

The difference, I think, as you turn the car off, is this: the starlight never knew where to look. It spun up enough energy to become light, shot through all that space and time, hoping to land on someone that cared enough to look up and see it. And if it missed watching eyes, that was it. The missed connection was just that: missed.

But boy, sweetheart, did I see you.

I know you saw me too.

That'll be what I'll carry, in varying weight in my bones, as we move on and keep becoming the people we're supposed to be. As the space grows, quite literally, but also in the sinew between our veins, the places in our bodies that keep us moving in opposite directions. I know you'll feel the tug sometimes, to call. To check. I'll wonder about you too, and hope you're okay. I'll always wonder. But it's time to get out of the car.

Your fingers knot into fists in the parking lot. "I feel like I'm not going to see you again."

I rush to you, tucking my chin into your shoulder. Your hands dance across my back, as if your fingers can't decide where to land. "Yes, you will. Of course you will," I say. In our hug, you don't have to watch me lie to you in our last moment together.

Your hands still, and you cling. The fog rises off the river below us, and I count. My arm over your shoulder, fingers in your hair and clutching your black t-shirt. Your arms hold me against you. Your forehead in my neck. Your heart hammers inside you. Mine probably is too.

The gust of air that parts us, as humid as it is, is the coldest thing I've ever felt.

But your smile is back. Maybe for you, maybe for me. It doesn't matter. It's brighter than sunshine.

I was the luckiest human in the universe to know you.

You wave as my blinker ticks right, to take me away, to where every single thing will be the exact same, but entirely different, again. Go. Go.

Gone.

# Thank you.

Mom and Dad: thank you. I'm so grateful you gave me the space then to figure myself out....and then gave me every notebook I asked for to fill while I did it.

Spencer, you're my biggest fan, and I'm yours. Always.

Amanda. The best to my friend. The weeble to my wobble. Love you more than taco-flavored kisses.

Jessica. I am better for having you and your kind heart only a text away.

Sam. When I wrote this, I didn't know yet, but you are the only thing brighter to me than the sun. Love you always, more than everything.

Brett. For being the moon to Sam's sun. You steady my axis and give me comfort in the shadows. BBBG.

And, little me. This was a long time coming. That girl under the lace curtains, watching the windows breathe, is so, so, so proud of you.

# About the Author

STEPHANIE LOGUE is a non-fiction and fiction writer living in South Dakota with her husband and son. She has one completed young adult novel, and is working on her first new adult novel, both featuring women figuring it out in South Dakota. In her free time, Stephanie listens to Taylor Swift, drafts bookish business plans and novel outlines inspired by country music from the 2000's at her favorite table in Coffea in Sioux Falls.

Stephanie can be found on Instagram @stephanielogue_writes.